Read more Kung Pow Chicken books!

1

2

3

4

POW CHICKEN★

HEROES ON THE SIDE

Cyndi Marko

⬥⬦ BRANCHES ⬦⬥

SCHOLASTIC INC.

For Lucian
Guess what? Chicken butt

Library of Congress Cataloging-in-Publication Data
Marko, Cyndi, author, illustrator.
Heroes on the side / by Cyndi Marko.
pages cm. — (Kung Pow Chicken ; 4)
Summary: When the Blue family travels to New Yolk City, Egg Drop wants to go to
the first-ever Sidekick Super-Con—a big party for sidekicks—but Ticklebeak and his Bad
Eggs soon chicknap the sidekicks and it is up to Kung Pow Chicken to save them.
ISBN 0-545-61074-5 (pbk.) — ISBN 0-545-61077-X (hardcover) — ISBN
0-545-61395-7 (ebook) [1. Superheroes—Fiction. 2. Chickens—Fiction. 3.
Kidnapping—Fiction. 4. Humorous stories.] I. Title.
PZ7.M33968Her 2014
[Fic]—dc23

2014017066

ISBN 978-0-545-61077-3 (hardcover) / ISBN 978-0-545-61074-2 (paperback)

10 9 8 7 6 5 4 3 2   18 19 20 21 22 23/0

Printed in China   6

First Scholastic printing, December 2014

TABLE OF CONTENTS

pirate ship

first mate

city of
Vladelphia

pirate
sword

comb

wattle

pirate sash

tail feathers

buried treasure
(lunch box)

Gordon Blue seemed like an ordinary chicken.

Gordon had an ordinary family. (Most of the time.)

And he liked ordinary things.

my favorite comic.

I ♡ my bike.

I caught a fish!

But Gordon had a <u>super</u> secret.

Uncle Quack was the <u>only</u> chicken who knew Gordon's <u>super</u> secret. And everyone knew that Uncle Quack helped Kung Pow Chicken catch bad guys.

Gordon liked having superpowers. But it was <u>super</u> hard being a superhero.

Gordon's mom called when he was battling bad guys.

Some people thought anyone could be a superhero.

And he had to put up with a cheeky sidekick.

Gordon loved chasing bad guys in his city. But today, the Blue family was getting ready to go on a trip to New Yolk City.

New Yolk has the _best_ superhero! I hope I'll get to meet Rubber Rooster. He's super cool!

So is his sidekick, Radar!

How does Rubber Rooster keep his leotard from sticking?

Gordon and Benny went to the lab to help their uncle pack.

Um, I don't think there's room for that.

I can't wait to go skating in New Yolk!

Oh! I almost forgot! A flyer came in the mail for Egg Drop.

Benny took the flyer from Uncle Quack.

SIDEKICK SUPER★CON!

Dear Egg Drop,
  You are invited to a party! Radar, sidekick to NYC's Rubber Rooster, is proud to host the FIRST-EVER SIDEKICK SUPER-CON! Eat yummy lunch and dessert! Dance and play games with other sidekicks! And see who will win the SIDEKICK OF THE YEAR award!

★ **WHEN:** Saturday at 1 PM
★★ **WHERE:** Birdy Ballroom

Gordon and Benny went home to do their own packing.

The boys were too excited to sleep.

On Friday morning, the Blue family boarded a plane to New Yolk City!

They all dropped off their luggage at the Roostervelt Hotel.

Then Mrs. Blue dashed off to the fancy shops. And Uncle Quack took his nephews ice-skating.

They were all having fun on the ice.

Suddenly, Gordon's tail feathers started to tingle. He knew what that meant: A bad guy was up to no good!

The brothers found a good place to hide. Gordon flung open his lunch box and grabbed his super suit. Benny put on his mask.

Just then, <u>another</u> superhero team burst onto the ice.

Gordon squeezed into his leotard. But he was too late. Rubber Rooster and Radar had chased the bad guys away.

Rubber Rooster was swarmed by star-struck chickens. Kung Pow Chicken wanted to meet him. But he couldn't get through the crowd.

No one's ever asked _you_ to sign anything.

New Yolk is Rubber Rooster's city. Let him catch the bad guys.

Gordon and Benny stayed in the hotel room for the rest of the day. Gordon moped. Benny daydreamed.

I'd like to thank Professor Quack. And my good friend Beak Girl.

Early Saturday morning, Gordon and his family went sight-seeing all over New Yolk City.

Then it was almost time for Sidekick Super-Con!
Uncle Quack had a plan to keep Mrs. Blue busy.
He was taking her to the spa for an afternoon of
pampering.

Benny was ready to go in a jiffy. But Gordon wanted to look <u>extra</u> super in case he ran into other superheroes.

By the time Gordon was ready, Benny was in a tizzy.

They rushed out of the room and down the hall.

Gordon hummed along with the elevator music.

Then they scrambled through the lobby.

And the doorman hailed them a cab.

BOK!

HOTEL

The cab headed to Sidekick Super-Con.
Gordon was excited to visit the Statue of Libirdy
after he dropped off Benny.

Breaking news! Escaped feathered funny guy,
Ticklebeak, and his crew of Bad Eggs, have taken
over the Birdy Ballroom! Sidekicks from all over
the world, who just came here to party, are now
trapped inside! What will our city's superhero,
Rubber Rooster, do? And will visiting
superheroes help out?

Now, aren't you glad we're late?
Or you'd be trapped, too!

We have to help the
trapped sidekicks!

The cab zoomed in and out of traffic. Gordon and Benny bokked about the trapped sidekicks.

The cab skidded to a stop near the Birdy Ballroom. Gordon paid the taxi driver.

They put on their super suits.

Kung Pow Chicken jumped out, ready to battle! Egg Drop was already off and running.

Two Bad Eggs stood guard. The heroes tiptoed around the building to look for another way in.

Kung Pow Chicken slipped around the corner.
He crashed into another hero.

But Rubber Rooster and Kung Pow Chicken did not seem to notice Egg Drop. They had important <u>super</u> stuff to talk about.

Wow. I really like your leotard.

Thanks. I made it myself.

Do you have a problem with wedgies?

Oh, for peep's sake.

Soon more superheroes showed up. They all had sidekicks trapped in the Birdy Ballroom.

While the superheroes were busy bokking, Ticklebeak and some Bad Eggs tried to sneak away. One of the Bad Eggs giggled.

The good guys got in a super-mega battle
with the bad guys!

KAPOW!

giggle

giggle

BOING!

giggle

DRUMSTICKS
OF
DOOM!

The battle raged on and on.

But the bad guys got away.

The other superheroes went off after the bad guys. But Kung Pow Chicken and Egg Drop were hungry.

The heroes ate pie and tried to figure out what to do next.

This pie is really good.

You've got berries on your beak.

RIIIING!!

Kung Pow Chicken answered his Beak-Phone.

It was Uncle Quack.

Kung Pow Chicken put away his phone.

The heroes rushed to the subway.

The Bad Eggs had been busy. They had hit all the hot spots in the city: the Statue of Libirdy, the New Yolk Public Library, and even Rockefeather Center.

First, Kung Pow Chicken and Egg Drop went to the Statue of Libirdy.

The Statue of Libirdy doesn't wear bloomers!

It's pretty funny though.

tee hee hee

The Bad Eggs had made a mess of the statue. But they hadn't left any clues to where Ticklebeak could be.

Next, the heroes went to the public library.

Then Kung Pow Chicken and Egg Drop went back to Rockefeather Center. Now the ice rink was filled with gooey white stuff.

The superheroes searched high and low. Finally, they spotted a clue.

As soon as the heroes reached the museum,
Kung Pow Chicken's tail feathers started to tingle.
Then Kung Pow Chicken and Egg Drop heard
goofy giggling. They hid.

Ticklebeak and some Bad Eggs! What were they doing in the museum?

EGGENHEIM MUSEUM

giggle

giggle

Look! Ticklebeak has the Fancy-pants Gold Egg!

45

Kung Pow Chicken and Egg Drop followed
Ticklebeak and the Bad Eggs all the way to
Times Oval.

Times Oval was full of Bad Eggs. They were making a mess.

Just then, the other superheroes showed up.
Kung Pow Chicken waved them over.

What do we do?

We fight!

Yes!

Egg Drop, stay here. You'll just be in our way.

Hmph. That was <u>super</u> mean.

Egg Drop watched the superheroes fight with all their might.

Then he watched them all get caught! Without their sidekicks, the heroes were easily trapped.

A Bad Egg sprayed Kung Pow Chicken's beak shut with Super-Silly String.

Egg Drop had to free the superheroes. But he needed help. He needed sidekicks.

Egg Drop slipped away. He rushed back to the hotel. Uncle Quack would know what to do.

Ticklebeak and his Bad Eggs have chick-napped Gordon—and the other superheroes, too! I'm the <u>only</u> one who can save them!

And, um, I don't think those cucumbers are for eating.

HOTEL SPA "FOR PUFFY EYES"

Uncle Quack had been busy working on a new gadget.

This gadget should help you rescue the sidekicks. It's a super disguise called the Pi-ZZZ-a Guy™. I baked a yummy cheesy pizza. And I warmed a jug of milk. Together, these should make those Bad Eggs super sleepy!

I'll keep your mom busy at the spa. Good luck.

Thanks!

Egg Drop pedaled the bicycle taxi to the Birdy Ballroom. Then he took a big breath and climbed up the front steps.

The Bad Eggs shrugged. They gobbled up the pizza. They gulped down the warm milk. Then their tummies were full and they fell asleep.

Egg Drop grabbed the key and unlocked the door.

The sidekicks were very happy to see Egg Drop.

Egg Drop had a plan. He told it to the sidekicks.
Then they took the subway to Times Oval.

The sidekicks burst up out of the subway.

They jumped right into battle with Ticklebeak's Bad Eggs.

Egg Drop and Radar slipped away from the fight. They ran over to free the superheroes. Egg Drop scraped the Super-Silly String from Kung Pow Chicken's beak.

Kung Pow, use your Power Peck!

PECK! PECK

The superheroes were free of Ticklebeak's messy trap in no time.

Good work, Radar!

You, too, Egg Drop! But what took you so long? Now, let's get cracking!

The big battle continued. Then Ticklebeak stepped forward. He bokked loudly. Everyone stopped fighting so they could hear better.

But jail was no fun. Ticklebeak would not go back without a fight! Kung Pow Chicken flashed his Drumsticks of Doom.

The Bad Eggs rushed at the superheroes. The heroes were outnumbered.

But the sidekicks were ready! They tossed rolls of Ultra-Mega Toilet Paper to their superheroes. And they sprayed cans of Super-Silly String.

ZZZZZIP!

OF MICE AND CHICKENS

SPISH!

SPISH!

The sidekicks and superheroes put Ticklebeak and all of his Bad Eggs in one basket.

The good guys said their good-byes. Radar gave Egg Drop a high five.

Kung Pow Chicken and Egg Drop took off
their super suits and ran back to the hotel.
Mrs. Blue gave her boys a big hug.

The next morning, the Blue family flew home
to Fowladelphia. Gordon and Benny went with
Uncle Quack to the lab. A surprise was waiting
for Egg Drop.

WANTED

FOR BEING SILLY!

← funny disguise

Cyndi Marko lives in Canada with her family.

When Cyndi was younger, she thought she was <u>so</u> funny. She loved to tell jokes to make her friends laugh. She would sneak up on her dad to scare him, giggling the whole time. And when guests came over, she would tell them her mom had made slime soup for dinner. (It was split green-pea soup! Pretty slimy, right? Ew!) Now that Cyndi is older, she—well, she still thinks she's pretty funny.

Kung Pow Chicken is Cyndi's first children's book series.

← green slime soup

split peas

BIG BOOK OF JOKES

KUNG POW CHICKEN

Prove your superhero know-how!

Why does Gordon think it is super hard being a superhero?

Why does Ticklebeak make the Bad Eggs do pranks all over the city?

Draw pictures and write speech bubbles to retell the important events of <u>Heroes on the Side</u>.

How does Uncle Quack's gadget help Egg Drop rescue the sidekicks?

Egg Drop has just won the award for Sidekick of the Year. Write an acceptance speech for him!